OSCAR WILDE

THE PORTRAIT OF MR W. H.

PENGUIN BOOKS

PENGUIN BOOKS

Published by the Penguin Group
Penguin Books Ltd, 27 Wrights Lane, London w8 5tz, England
Penguin Books USA Inc., 375 Hudson Street, New York, New York 10014, USA
Penguin Books Australia Ltd, Ringwood, Victoria, Australia
Penguin Books Canada Ltd, 10 Alcorn Avenue, Toronto, Ontario, Canada m4v 3b2
Penguin Books (NZ) Ltd, 182–190 Wairau Road, Auckland 10, New Zealand

Penguin Books Ltd, Registered Offices: Harmondsworth, Middlesex, England

These extracts are from *The Complete Short Fiction of Oscar Wilde*,
edited by Ian Small, first published in Penguin Classics 1994, and
The Portable Oscar Wilde, edited by Richard Aldington and Stanley Weintraub,
revised edition published in Penguin Books 1981
This edition published 1995
1 3 5 7 9 10 8 6 4 2

Copyright © Ian Small, 1994; Viking Penguin, Inc., 1981
All rights reserved

The moral right of the editor of *The Complete Short
Fiction of Oscar Wilde* has been asserted

Typeset by Rowland Phototypesetting Ltd, Bury St Edmunds, Suffolk
Printed in England by Clays Ltd, St Ives plc

CONTENTS

The Portrait of Mr W. H.

I had been dining with Erskine in his pretty little house in Birdcage Walk, and we were sitting in the library over our coffee and cigarettes, when the question of literary forgeries happened to turn up in conversation. I cannot at present remember how it was that we stuck upon this somewhat curious topic, as it was at that time, but I know that we had a long discussion about Macpherson, Ireland, and Chatterton, and that with regard to the last I insisted that his so-called forgeries were merely the result of an artistic desire for perfect representation; that we had no right to quarrel with an artist for the conditions under which he chooses to present his work; and that all Art being to a certain degree a mode of acting, an attempt to realize one's own personality on some imaginative plane out of reach of the trammelling accidents and limitations of real life, to censure an artist for a forgery was to confuse an ethical with an aesthetical problem.

Erskine, who was a good deal older than I was, and had been listening to me with the amused deference of a man of forty, suddenly put his hand upon my shoulder and said to me, 'What would you say about a young man who had a strange theory about a certain work of art, believed in his theory, and committed a forgery in order to prove it?'

'Ah! that is quite a different matter,' I answered.

Erskine remained silent for a few moments, looking at the thin grey threads of smoke that were rising from his cigarette. 'Yes,' he said, after a pause, 'quite different.'

There was something in the tone of his voice, a slight touch of bitterness perhaps, that excited my curiosity. 'Did you ever know anybody who did that?' I cried.

'Yes,' he answered, throwing his cigarette into the fire, — 'a great friend of mine, Cyril Graham. He was very fascinating, and very foolish, and very heartless. However, he left me the only legacy I ever received in my life.'

'What was that?' I exclaimed. Erskine rose from his seat, and going over to a tall inlaid cabinet that stood between the two windows, unlocked it, and came back to where I was sitting, holding in his hand a small panel picture set in an old and somewhat tarnished Elizabethan frame.

It was a full-length portrait of a young man in late sixteenth-century costume, standing by a table, with his right hand resting on an open book. He seemed about seventeen years of age, and was of quite extraordinary personal beauty, though evidently somewhat effeminate. Indeed, had it not been for the dress and the closely cropped hair, one would have said that the face, with its dreamy wistful eyes, and its delicate scarlet lips, was the face of a girl. In manner, and especially in the treatment of the hands, the picture reminded one of François Clouet's later work. The black velvet doublet with its fantastically gilded points, and the peacock-blue background against which it showed up so pleasantly, and from which it gained such luminous value of colour, were quite in Clouet's style; and the two masks of Tragedy and Comedy that hung somewhat formally from the marble pedestal had that hard severity of touch — so different from the facile grace of the Italians —

3

which even at the Court of France the great Flemish master never completely lost, and which in itself has always been a characteristic of the northern temper.

'It is a charming thing,' I cried; 'but who is this wonderful young man, whose beauty Art has so happily preserved for us?'

'This is the portrait of Mr W. H.,' said Erskine, with a sad smile. It might have been a chance effect of light, but it seemed to me that his eyes were quite bright with tears.

'Mr W. H.!' I exclaimed; 'who was Mr W. H.?'

'Don't you remember?' he answered. 'Look at the book on which his hand is resting.'

'I see there is some writing there, but I cannot make it out,' I replied.

'Take this magnifying-glass and try,' said Erskine, with the same sad smile still playing about his mouth.

I took the glass, and moving the lamp a little nearer, I began to spell out the crabbed sixteenth-century handwriting. 'To the onlie begetter of these insuing sonnets' . . . 'Good heavens!' I cried. 'Is this Shakespeare's Mr W. H.?'

'Cyril Graham used to say so,' muttered Erskine.

'But it is not a bit like Lord Pembroke,' I answered. 'I know the Penshurst portraits very well. I was staying near there a few weeks ago.'

'Do you really believe then that the Sonnets are addressed to Lord Pembroke?' he asked.

'I am sure of it,' I answered. 'Pembroke, Shakespeare, and Mrs Mary Fitton are the three personages of the Sonnets; there is no doubt at all about it.'

'Well, I agree with you,' said Erskine, 'but I did not always think so. I used to believe – well, I suppose I used to believe in Cyril Graham and his theory.'

'And what was that?' I asked, looking at the wonderful portrait, which had already begun to have a strange fascination for me.

'It is a long story,' said Erskine, taking the picture away from me – rather abruptly I thought at the time – 'a very long story; but if you care to hear it, I will tell it to you.'

'I love theories about the Sonnets,' I cried; 'but I don't think I am likely to be converted to any new idea. The matter has ceased to be a mystery to any one. Indeed, I wonder that it ever was a mystery.'

'As I don't believe in the theory, I am not likely to convert you to it,' said Erskine, laughing; 'but it may interest you.'

'Tell it to me, of course,' I answered. 'If it is half as delightful as the picture, I shall be more than satisfied.'

'Well,' said Erskine, lighting a cigarette, 'I must begin by telling you about Cyril Graham himself. He and I were at the same house at Eton. I was a year or two older than he was, but we were immense friends, and did all our work and all our play together. There was, of course, a good deal more play than work, but I cannot say that I am sorry for that. It is always an advantage not to have received a sound commercial education, and what I learned in the playing fields at Eton has been quite as useful to me as anything I was taught at Cambridge. I should tell you that Cyril's father and mother were both dead. They had been drowned in a horrible yachting accident off the Isle of Wight. His father had been in the diplomatic service, and had married a daughter, the only daughter, in fact, of old Lord Crediton, who became Cyril's guardian after the death of his parents. I don't think that Lord Crediton cared very much for Cyril. He had never really forgiven his daughter for marrying a man who had no title. He was an extraordinary old aristocrat, who swore like a costermonger, and had the manners of a farmer. I remember seeing him once on Speech-day. He growled at me, gave me a sovereign, and told me not to grow up "a damned Radical" like my father. Cyril had very little affection for him, and was only too glad to spend most of his holidays with us in Scotland. They never really got on together at all. Cyril thought him a bear, and he thought Cyril effeminate. He was effeminate, I suppose, in some things, though he was a very good rider and a capital fencer. In fact he got the foils before he left Eton. But he was very languid in his manner, and not a little vain of his good looks, and had a strong objection to football. The two things that really gave him pleasure were poetry and acting. At Eton he was always dressing up and reciting Shakespeare, and when he went up to Trinity he became a member of the ADC his first term. I remember I was always very jealous of his acting. I was absurdly devoted to him; I suppose because we were so different in some things. I was a rather awkward, weakly lad, with huge feet, and horribly freckled. Freckles run in Scotch families just as gout does in English families. Cyril used to say that of the two he preferred the gout; but he always set an absurdly high value on personal appearance, and once read a paper before our debating society to prove that it was better to be good-looking than to be good. He certainly was wonderfully handsome. People who did not like him, Philistines, and college tutors, and young men reading for the Church, used to say that he was merely pretty; but there was a great deal more in his face than mere prettiness. I think he was the most splendid creature I ever saw, and nothing could exceed the grace of his movements, the charm of his manner. He fascinated everybody who was worth fascinating, and a great many people who were not. He was often wilful and petulant, and I used to think him dreadfully insincere. It was due, I think, chiefly to his inordinate desire to please. Poor Cyril! I told him once that he was contented with very cheap triumphs, but he only laughed. He was horribly spoiled. All charming people, I fancy, are spoiled. It is the secret of their attraction.

'However, I must tell you about Cyril's acting. You know that no actresses are allowed to play at the ADC. At least they were not in my time, I don't know how it is now. Well, of course Cyril was always cast for the girls' parts, and when *As You Like It* was produced he played Rosalind. It was a marvellous performance. In fact, Cyril Graham was the only perfect Rosalind I have ever seen. It would be impossible to describe to you the beauty, the delicacy, the refinement of the whole thing. It made an immense sensation, and the horrid little theatre, as it was then, was crowded every night. Even when I read the play now I can't help thinking of Cyril. It might have been written for him. The next term he took his degree, and came to London to read for the diplomatic. But he never did any work. He spent his days in reading Shakespeare's Sonnets, and his evenings at the theatre. He was, of course, wild to go on the stage. It was all that I and Lord Crediton could do to prevent him. Perhaps if he had gone on the stage he would be alive now. It is always a silly thing to give advice, but to give good advice is absolutely fatal. I hope you will never fall into that error. If you do, you will be sorry for it.

'Well, to come to the real point of the story, one day I got a letter from Cyril asking me to come round to his rooms that evening. He had charming chambers in Piccadilly overlooking the Green Park, and as I used to go to see him every day, I was rather surprised at his taking the trouble to write. Of course I went, and when I arrived I found him in a state of great excitement. He told me that he had at last discovered the true secret of Shakespeare's Sonnets; that all the scholars and critics had been entirely on the wrong tack; and that he was the first who, working purely by internal evidence, had found out who Mr W. H. really was. He was perfectly wild with delight, and for a long time would not tell me his theory. Finally, he produced a bundle of notes, took his copy of the Sonnets off the mantelpiece, and sat down and gave me a long lecture on the whole subject.

'He began by pointing out that the young man to

whom Shakespeare addressed these strangely passionate poems must have been somebody who was a really vital factor in the development of his dramatic art, and that this could not be said either of Lord Pembroke or Lord Southampton. Indeed, whoever he was, he could not have been anybody of high birth, as was shown very clearly by the 25th Sonnet, in which Shakespeare contrasts himself with those who are "great princes' favourites"; says quite frankly

> Let those who are in favour with their stars
> Of public honour and proud titles boast,
> Whilst I, whom fortune of such triumph bars,
> Unlook'd for joy in that I honour most;

and ends the sonnet by congratulating himself on the mean state of him he so adored:

> Then happy I, that loved and am beloved
> Where I may not remove nor be removed.

This sonnet, Cyril declared, would be quite unintelligible if we fancied that it was addressed to either the Earl of Pembroke or the Earl of Southampton, both of whom were men of the highest position in England and fully entitled to be called "great princes"; and he in corroboration of his view read me Sonnets CXXIV and CXXV, in which Shakespeare tells us that his love is not "the child of state", that it "suffers not in smiling pomp", but is "builded far from accident". I listened with a good deal of interest, for I don't think the point had ever been made before; but what followed was still more curious, and seemed to me at the time to entirely dispose of Pembroke's claim. We know from Meres that the Sonnets had been written before 1598, and Sonnet CIV informs us that Shakespeare's friendship for Mr W. H. had been already in existence for three years. Now Lord Pembroke, who was born in 1580, did not come to London till he was eighteen years of age, that is to say till 1598, and Shakespeare's acquaintance with Mr W. H. must have begun in 1594, or at the latest in 1595. Shakespeare, accordingly, could not have known Lord Pembroke till after the Sonnets had been written.

'Cyril pointed out also that Pembroke's father did not die till 1601; whereas it was evident from the line

that the father of Mr W. H. was dead in 1598.
Besides, it was absurd to imagine that any publisher of the time, and the preface is from the
publisher's hand, would have ventured to address
William Herbert, Earl of Pembroke, as Mr W. H.;
the case of Lord Buckhurst being spoken of as Mr
Sackville being not really a parallel instance, as
Lord Buckhurst was not a peer, but merely the
younger son of a peer, with a courtesy title, and the
passage in *England's Parnassus*, where he is so
spoken of, is not a formal and stately dedication,
but simply a casual allusion. So far for Lord
Pembroke, whose supposed claims Cyril easily
demolished while I sat by in wonder. With Lord
Southampton Cyril had even less difficulty. Southampton became at a very early age the lover of
Elizabeth Vernon, so he needed no entreaties to
marry; he was not beautiful; he did not resemble
his mother, as Mr W. H. did —

Thou art thy mother's glass, and she in thee
Calls back the lovely April of her prime;

and, above all, his Christian name was Henry, whereas the punning sonnets (CXXXV and CXLIII) show that the Christian name of Shakespeare's friend was the same as his own – *Will*.

'As for the other suggestions of unfortunate commentators, that Mr W. H. is a misprint for Mr W. S., meaning Mr William Shakespeare; that "Mr W. H. all" should be read "Mr W. Hall"; that Mr W. H. is Mr William Hathaway; and that a full stop should be placed after "wisheth", making Mr W. H. the writer and not the subject of the dedication, – Cyril got rid of them in a very short time; and it is not worth while to mention his reasons, though I remember he sent me off into a fit of laughter by reading to me, I am glad to say not in the original, some extracts from a German commentator called Barnstorff, who insisted that Mr W. H. was no less a person than "Mr William Himself". Nor would he allow for a moment that the Sonnets are mere satires on the work of Drayton and John Davies of Hereford. To him, as indeed to me, they were poems of serious and tragic import, wrung out of the bitterness of Shakespeare's heart, and made sweet by the honey of his lips. Still less would he admit that they were merely a philosophical allegory, and that in them Shakespeare is addressing his Ideal Self, or Ideal Manhood, or the Spirit of Beauty, or the Reason, or the Divine Logos, or the Catholic Church. He felt, as indeed I think we all must feel, that the Sonnets are addressed to an individual, — to a particular young man whose personality for some reason seems to have filled the soul of Shakespeare with terrible joy and no less terrible despair.

'Having in this manner cleared the way as it were, Cyril asked me to dismiss from my mind any preconceived ideas I might have formed on the subject, and to give a fair and unbiased hearing to his own theory. The problem he pointed out was this: who was that young man of Shakespeare's day who, without being of noble birth or even of noble nature, was addressed by him in terms of such passionate adoration that we can but wonder at the strange worship, and are almost afraid to turn the key that unlocks the mystery of the poet's heart? Who was he whose physical beauty was such that it became the very corner-stone of Shakespeare's art; the very source of Shakespeare's inspiration; the very incarnation of Shakespeare's dreams? To look upon him as simply the object of certain love-poems is to miss the whole meaning of the poems: for the art of which Shakespeare talks in the Sonnets is not the art of the Sonnets themselves, which indeed were to him but slight and secret things — it is the art of the dramatist to which he is always alluding; and he to whom Shakespeare said —

> Though art all my art, and dost advance
> As high as learning my rude ignorance,

he to whom he promised immortality,

Where breath most breathes, even in the mouth of men,

was surely none other than the boy-actor for whom he created Viola and Imogen, Juliet and Rosalind, Portia and Desdemona, and Cleopatra herself. This was Cyril Graham's theory, evolved as you see purely from the Sonnets themselves, and depending for its acceptance, not so much on demonstrable proof or formal evidence, but on a kind of spiritual and artistic sense, by which alone he claimed could the true meaning of the poems be discerned. I remember his reading to me that fine sonnet —

How can my Muse want subject to invent,
While thou dost breathe, that pour'st into my verse
Thine own sweet argument, too excellent
For every vulgar paper to rehearse?
O, give thyself the thanks, if aught in me
Worthy perusal stand against thy sight;
For who's so dumb that cannot write to thee,
When thou thyself dost give invention light?
Be thou the tenth Muse, ten times more in worth
Than those old nine which rhymers invocate;
And he that calls on thee, let him bring forth
Eternal numbers to outlive long date

— and pointing out how completely it corroborated his theory; and indeed he went through all the Sonnets carefully, and showed, or fancied that he showed, that, according to his new explanation of their meaning, things that had seemed obscure, or evil, or exaggerated, became clear and rational, and of high artistic import, illustrating Shakespeare's conception of the true relations between the art of the actor and the art of the dramatist.

'It is of course evident that there must have been

in Shakespeare's company some wonderful boy-actor of great beauty, to whom he intrusted the presentation of his noble heroines; for Shakespeare was a practical theatrical manager as well as an imaginative poet, and Cyril Graham had actually discovered the boy-actor's name. He was Will, or, as he preferred to call him, Willie Hughes. The Christian name he found of course in the punning sonnets, CXXXV and CXLIII; the surname was, according to him, hidden in the eighth line of the 20th Sonnet, where Mr W. H. is described as —

A man in hew, all *Hews* in his controwling.

'In the original edition of the Sonnets "Hews" is printed with a capital letter and in italics, and this, he claimed, showed clearly that a play on words was intended, his view receiving a good deal of corroboration from those sonnets in which curious puns are made on the words "use" and "usury". Of course I was converted at once, and Willie Hughes became to me as real a person as Shakespeare. The only objection I made to the theory was that the name of Willie Hughes does not occur in the list of the actors of Shakespeare's company as it is printed in the first folio. Cyril, however, pointed out that the absence of Willie Hughes's name from this list really corroborated the theory, as it was evident from Sonnet LXXXVI that Willie Hughes had abandoned Shakespeare's company to play at a rival theatre, probably in some of Chapman's plays. It is in reference to this that in the great sonnet on Chapman Shakespeare said to Willie Hughes –

But when your countenance filled up his line,
Then lacked I matter; that enfeebled mine –

the expression "when your countenance filled up his line" referring obviously to the beauty of the young actor giving life and reality and added charm to Chapman's verse, the same idea being also put forward in the 79th Sonnet –

Whilst I alone did call upon thy aid,
My verse alone had all thy gentle grace,
But now my gracious numbers are decayed,
And my sick Muse does give another place;

and in the immediately preceding sonnet, where
Shakespeare says

> Every alien pen has got my *use*
> And under thee their poesy disperse,

the play upon words (use = Hughes) being of
course obvious, and the phrase "under thee their
poesy disperse", meaning "by your assistance as
an actor bring their plays before the people".

'It was a wonderful evening, and we sat up
almost till dawn reading and re-reading the Sonnets. After some time, however, I began to see that
before the theory could be placed before the world
in a really perfected form, it was necessary to get
some independent evidence about the existence of
this young actor Willie Hughes. If this could be
once established, there could be no possible doubt
about his identity with Mr W. H.; but otherwise
the theory would fall to the ground. I put this
forward very strongly to Cyril, who was a good
deal annoyed at what he called my Philistine tone
of mind, and indeed was rather bitter upon the
subject. However, I made him promise that in his
own interest he would not publish his discovery till

he had put the whole matter beyond the reach of doubt; and for weeks and weeks we searched the registers of City churches, the Alleyn MSS at Dulwich, the Record Office, the papers of the Lord Chamberlain — everything, in fact, that we thought might contain some allusion to Willie Hughes. We discovered nothing, of course, and every day the existence of Willie Hughes seemed to me to become more problematical. Cyril was in a dreadful state, and used to go over the whole question day after day, entreating me to believe; but I saw the one flaw in the theory, and I refused to be convinced till the actual existence of Willie Hughes, a boy-actor of Elizabethan days, had been placed beyond the reach of doubt or cavil.

'One day Cyril left town to stay with his grandfather, I thought at the time, but I afterwards heard from Lord Crediton that this was not the case; and about a fortnight afterwards I received a telegram from him, handed in at Warwick, asking me to be sure to come and dine with him that evening at eight o'clock. When I arrived, he said to me, "The only apostle who did not deserve proof was S. Thomas, and S. Thomas was the only apostle who got it." I asked him what he meant. He answered that he had not merely been able to establish the existence in the sixteenth century of a boy-actor of the name of Willie Hughes, but to prove by the most conclusive evidence that he was the Mr W. H. of the Sonnets. He would not tell me anything more at the time; but after dinner he solemnly produced the picture I showed you, and told me that he had discovered it by the merest chance nailed to the side of an old chest that he had bought at a farmhouse in Warwickshire. The chest itself, which was a very fine example of Elizabethan work, he had, of course, brought with him, and in the centre of the front panel the initials W. H. were undoubtedly carved. It was this monogram that had attracted his attention, and he told me that it was not till he had had the chest in his possession for several days that he had thought of making any careful examination of the inside. One morning, however, he saw that one of the sides of the chest was much thicker than the other, and looking more closely, he discovered that a framed panel picture was clamped against it. On taking it out, he found it was the picture that is now lying on the sofa. It was very dirty, and covered with mould; but he managed to clean it, and, to his great joy, saw that he had fallen by mere chance on the one thing for which he had been looking. Here was an authentic portrait of Mr W. H., with his hand resting on the dedicatory page of the Sonnets, and on the frame itself could be faintly seen the name of the young man written in black uncial letters on a faded gold ground, "Master Will. Hews".

'Well, what was I to say? It never occurred to me for a moment that Cyril Graham was playing a trick on me, or that he was trying to prove his theory by means of a forgery.'

'But is it a forgery?' I asked.

'Of course it is,' said Erskine. 'It is a very good forgery; but it is a forgery none the less. I thought at the time that Cyril was rather calm about the whole matter; but I remember he more than once told me that he himself required no proof of the kind, and that he thought the theory complete without it. I laughed at him, and told him that without it the theory would fall to the ground, and I warmly congratulated him on the marvellous discovery. We then arranged that the picture should be etched or facsimiled, and placed as the frontispiece to Cyril's edition of the Sonnets; and for three months we did nothing but go over each poem line by line, till we had settled every difficulty of text or meaning. One unlucky day I was in a print-shop in Holborn, when I saw upon the counter some extremely beautiful drawings in silverpoint. I was so attracted by them that I bought them; and the proprietor of the place, a man called Rawlings, told me that they were done by a young painter of the name of Edward Merton, who was very clever, but as poor as a church mouse. I went to see Merton some days afterwards, having got his address from the print-seller, and found a pale, interesting young man, with a rather common-looking wife — his model, as I subsequently learned. I told him how much I admired his drawings, at which he seemed very pleased, and I asked him if he would show me some of his other work. As we were looking over a portfolio, full of really very lovely things, — for Merton had a most delicate and delightful touch, — I suddenly caught sight of a drawing of the picture of Mr W. H. There was no doubt whatever about it. It was almost a facsimile – the only difference being that the two masks of Tragedy and Comedy were not suspended from the marble table as they are in the picture, but were lying on the floor at the young man's feet. "Where on earth did you get that?" I said. He grew rather confused, and said – "Oh, that is nothing. I did not know it was in this portfolio. It is not a thing of any value." "It is what you did for Mr Cyril Graham," exclaimed his wife; "and if this gentleman wishes to buy it, let him have it." "For Mr Cyril Graham?" I repeated. "Did you paint the picture of Mr W. H.?" "I don't understand what you mean," he answered, growing very red. Well, the whole thing was quite dreadful. The wife let it all out. I gave her five pounds when I was going away. I can't bear to think of it now; but of course I was furious. I went off at once to Cyril's chambers, waited there for three hours before he came in, with that horrid lie staring me in the face, and told him I had discovered his forgery. He grew very pale, and said – "I did it purely for your sake. You would not be convinced in any other way. It does not affect the truth of the theory." "The truth of the theory!" – I exclaimed; "the less we talk about that the better. You never even believed in it yourself. If you had, you would not have committed a forgery to prove it." High words passed between us; we had a fearful quarrel. I daresay I was unjust. The next morning he was dead.'

'Dead!' I cried.

'Yes; he shot himself with a revolver. Some of the blood splashed upon the frame of the picture, just where the name had been painted. By the time I arrived – his servant had sent for me at once – the police were already there. He had left a letter for me, evidently written in the greatest agitation and distress of mind.'

'What was in it?' I asked.

'Oh, that he believed absolutely in Willie Hughes; that the forgery of the picture had been done simply as a concession to me, and did not in the slightest degree invalidate the truth of the theory; and that in order to show me how firm and flawless his faith in the whole thing was, he was going to offer his life as a sacrifice to the secret of the Sonnets. It was a foolish, mad letter. I remember he ended by saying that he intrusted to me the

Willie Hughes theory, and that it was for me to present it to the world, and to unlock the secret of Shakespeare's heart.'

'It is a most tragic story,' I cried; 'but why have you not carried out his wishes?'

Erskine shrugged his shoulders. 'Because it is a perfectly unsound theory from beginning to end,' he answered.

'My dear Erskine,' I said, getting up from my seat, 'you are entirely wrong about the whole matter. It is the only perfect key to Shakespeare's Sonnets that has ever been made. It is complete in every detail. I believe in Willie Hughes.'

'Don't say that,' said Erskine gravely; 'I believe there is something fatal about the idea, and intellectually there is nothing to be said for it. I have gone into the whole matter, and I assure you the theory is entirely fallacious. It is plausible up to a certain point. Then it stops. For heaven's sake, my dear boy, don't take up the subject of Willie Hughes. You will break your heart over it.'

'Erskine,' I answered, 'it is your duty to give this theory to the world. If you will not do it, I will. By keeping it back you wrong the memory of Cyril

Graham, the youngest and the most splendid of all the martyrs of literature. I entreat you to do him justice. He died for this thing, – don't let his death be in vain.'

Erskine looked at me in amazement. 'You are carried away by the sentiment of the whole story,' he said. 'You forget that a thing is not necessarily true because a man dies for it. I was devoted to Cyril Graham. His death was a horrible blow to me. I did not recover it for years. I don't think I have ever recovered it. But Willie Hughes? There is nothing in the idea of Willie Hughes. No such person ever existed. As for bringing the whole thing before the world – the world thinks that Cyril Graham shot himself by accident. The only proof of his suicide was contained in the letter to me, and of this letter the public never heard anything. To the present day Lord Crediton thinks that the whole thing was accidental.'

'Cyril Graham sacrificed his life to a great idea,' I answered; 'and if you will not tell of his martyrdom, tell at least of his faith.'

'His faith,' said Erskine, 'was fixed in a thing that was false, in a thing that was unsound, in a thing that no Shakespearian scholar would accept for a moment. The theory would be laughed at. Don't make a fool of yourself, and don't follow a trail that leads nowhere. You start by assuming the existence of the very person whose existence is the thing to be proved. Besides, everybody knows that the Sonnets were addressed to Lord Pembroke. The matter is settled once for all.'

'The matter is not settled!' I exclaimed. 'I will take up the theory where Cyril Graham left it, and I will prove to the world that he was right.'

'Silly boy!' said Erskine. 'Go home; it is after two, and don't think about Willie Hughes any more. I am sorry I told you anything about it, and very sorry indeed that I should have converted you to a thing in which I don't believe.'

'You have given me the key to the greatest mystery of modern literature,' I answered; 'and I shall not rest till I have made you recognize, till I have made everybody recognize, that Cyril Graham was the most subtle Shakespearian critic of our day.'

As I walked home through St James's Park the dawn was just breaking over London. The white swans were lying asleep on the polished lake, and the gaunt Palace looked purple against the pale-green sky. I thought of Cyril Graham, and my eyes filled with tears.

It was past twelve o'clock when I awoke, and the sun was streaming in through the curtains of my room in long slanting beams of dusty gold. I told my servant that I would be at home to no one: and after I had had a cup of chocolate and a *petit-pain*, I took down from the book-shelf my copy of Shakespeare's Sonnets, and began to go carefully through them. Every poem seemed to me to corroborate Cyril Graham's theory. I felt as if I had my hand upon Shakespeare's heart, and was counting each separate throb and pulse of passion. I thought of the wonderful boy-actor, and saw his face in every line.

Two sonnets, I remember, struck me particularly: they were the 53rd and the 67th. In the first of these, Shakespeare, complimenting Willie Hughes on the versatility of his acting, on his wide range of parts, a range extending from Rosalind to Juliet, and from Beatrice to Ophelia, says to him –

> What is your substance, whereof are you made,
> That millions of strange shadows on you tend?
> Since every one hath, every one, one shade,
> And you, but one, can every shadow lend —

lines that would be unintelligible if they were not addressed to an actor, for the word 'shadow' had in Shakespeare's day a technical meaning connected with the stage. 'The best in this kind are but shadows,' says Theseus of the actors, in the *Midsummer Night's Dream*, and there are many similar allusions in the literature of the day. These sonnets evidently belonged to the series in which Shakespeare discusses the nature of the actor's art, and of the strange and rare temperament that is essential to the perfect stage-player. 'How is it,' says Shakespeare to Willie Hughes, 'that you have so many personalities?' and then he goes on to point out that his beauty is such that it seems to realize every form and phase of fancy, to embody each dream of the creative imagination — an idea that is still further expanded in the sonnet that immediately follows, where, beginning with the fine thought,

> O, how much more doth beauty beauteous seem
> By that sweet ornament which *truth* doth give!

Shakespeare invites us to notice how the truth of acting, the truth of visible presentation on the stage, adds to the wonder of poetry, giving life to its loveliness, and actual reality to its ideal form. And yet, in the 67th Sonnet, Shakespeare calls upon Willie Hughes to abandon the stage with its artificiality, its false mimic life of painted face and unreal costume, its immoral influences and suggestions, its remoteness from the true world of noble action and sincere utterance.

> Ah! wherefore with infection should he live,
> And with his presence grace impiety,
> That sin by him advantage should achieve,
> And lace itself with his society?
> Why should false painting imitate his cheek
> And steal dead seeming of his living hue?
> Why should poor beauty indirectly seek
> Roses of shadow, since his rose is true?'

It may seem strange that so great a dramatist as Shakespeare, who realized his own perfection as an artist and his humanity as a man on the ideal plane of stage-writing and stage-playing, should have written in these terms about the theatre; but we must remember in Sonnets CX and CXI Shakespeare shows us that he too was wearied of the world of puppets, and full of shame at having made himself 'a motley to the view'. The 111th Sonnet is especially bitter: —

O, for my sake do you with Fortune chide
The guilty goddess of my harmful deeds,
That did not better for my life provide
Than public means which public manners breeds.
Thence comes it that my name receives a brand,
And almost thence my nature is subdued
To what it works in, like the dyer's hand:
Pity me, then, and wish I were renewed —

and there are many signs elsewhere of the same feeling, signs familiar to all real students of Shakespeare.

One point puzzled me immensely as I read the Sonnets, and it was days before I struck on the true interpretation, which indeed Cyril Graham himself seems to have missed. I could not understand how it was that Shakespeare set so high a value on his young friend marrying. He himself had married young, and the result had been unhappiness, and it was not likely that he would have asked Willie Hughes to commit the same error. The boy-player of Rosalind had nothing to gain from marriage, or from the passions of real life. The early sonnets, with their strange entreaties to have children, seemed to me a jarring note. The explanation of the mystery came on me quite suddenly, and I found it in the curious dedication. It will be remembered that the dedication runs as follows:

TO THE ONLIE BEGETTER OF
THESE INSUING SONNETS
MR W. H. ALL HAPINESSE
AND THAT ETERNITIE
PROMISED BY
OUR EVER-LIVING POET
WISHETH
THE WELL-WISHING
ADVENTURER IN
SETTING
FORTH.

T. T.

Some scholars have supposed that the word 'be-getter' in this dedication means simply the pro-curer of the Sonnets for Thomas Thorpe the publisher; but this view is now generally aban-doned, and the highest authorities are quite agreed that it is to be taken in the sense of inspirer, the metaphor being drawn from the analogy of physi-cal life. Now I saw that the same metaphor was used by Shakespeare himself all through the poems, and this set me on the right track. Finally I made my great discovery. The marriage that Shakespeare proposes for Willie Hughes is the 'marriage with his Muse', an expression which is definitely put forward in the 82nd Sonnet, where, in the bitterness of his heart at the defection of the boy-actor for whom he had written his greatest parts, and whose beauty had indeed suggested them, he opens his complaint by saying —

I'll grant thou wert not married to my Muse.

The children he begs him to beget are no children of flesh and blood, but more immortal children of undying fame. The whole cycle of the early son-nets is simply Shakespeare's invitation to Willie

Hughes to go upon the stage and become a player. How barren and profitless a thing, he says, is this beauty of yours if it be not used: —

> When forty winters shall besiege thy brow,
> And dig deep trenches in thy beauty's field,
> Thy youth's proud livery, so gazed on now,
> Will be a tattered weed, of small worth held:
> Then being asked where all thy beauty lies,
> Where all the treasure of thy lusty days,
> To say, within thine own deep-sunken eyes,
> Were an all-eating shame and thriftless praise.

You must create something in art: my verse 'is thine, and *born* of thee'; only listen to me, and I will '*bring forth* eternal numbers to outlive long date', and you shall people with forms of your own image the imaginary world of the stage. These children that you beget, he continues, will not wither away, as mortal children do, but you shall live in them and in my plays: do but

> Make thee another self, for love of me,
> That beauty still may live in thine or thee!

I collected all the passages that seemed to me to corroborate this view, and they produced a strong impression on me, and showed me how complete Cyril Graham's theory really was. I also saw that it was quite easy to separate those lines in which he speaks of the Sonnets themselves from those in which he speaks of his great dramatic work. This was a point that had been entirely overlooked by all critics up to Cyril Graham's day. And yet it was one of the most important points in the whole series of poems. To the Sonnets Shakespeare was more or less indifferent. He did not wish to rest his fame on them. They were to him his 'slight Muse', as he calls them, and intended, as Meres tells us, for private circulation only among a few, a very few, friends. Upon the other hand he was extremely conscious of the high artistic value f his plays, and shows a noble self-reliance upon his dramatic genius. When he says to Willie Hughes: —

But thy eternal summer shall not fade,
Nor lose possession of that fair thou owest;
Nor shall Death brag thou wander'st in his shade,
When in *eternal lines* to time thou growest,
    So long as men can breathe or eyes can see,
    So long lives this and this gives life to thee;

the expression 'eternal lines' clearly alludes to one of his plays that he was sending him at the time, just as the concluding couplet points to his confidence in the probability of his plays being always acted. In his address to the Dramatic Muse (Sonnets C and CI), we find the same feeling.

Where art thou, Muse, that thou forget'st so long
To speak of that which gives thee all thy might?
Spends thou thy fury on some worthless song,
Darkening thy power to lend base subjects light?

he cries, and he then proceeds to reproach the mistress of Tragedy and Comedy for her 'neglect of Truth in Beauty dyed', and says —

Because he needs no praise, wilt thou be dumb?
Excuse not silence so; for 't lies in thee
To make him much outlive a gilded tomb,
And to be praised of ages yet to be.
    Then do thy office, Muse; I teach thee how
    To make him seem long hence as he shows now.

It is, however, perhaps in the 55th Sonnet that Shakespeare gives to this idea its fullest expression. To imagine that the 'powerful rhyme' of the second line refers to the sonnet itself, is to entirely

mistake Shakespeare's meaning. It seemed to me
that it was extremely likely, from the general
character of the sonnet, that a particular play was
meant, and that the play was none other but
Romeo and Juliet.

Not marble, nor the gilded monuments
Of princes, shall outlive this powerful rhyme;
But you shall shine more bright in these contents
Than unswept stone besmeared with sluttish time.
When wasteful wars shall statues overturn,
And broils root out the world of masonry,
Not Mars his sword nor war's quick fire shall burn
The living record of your memory.
'Gainst death and all-oblivious enmity
Shall you pace forth; your praise shall still find room
Even in the eyes of all posterity
That wear this world out to the ending doom.
    So, till the judgment that yourself arise,
      You live in this, and dwell in lovers' eyes.

It was also extremely suggestive to note how here
as elsewhere Shakespeare promised Willie Hughes
immortality in a form that appealed to men's eyes
– that is to say, in a spectacular form, in a play that
is to be looked at.

For two weeks I worked hard at the Sonnets, hardly ever going out, and refusing all invitations. Every day I seemed to be discovering something new, and Willie Hughes became to me a kind of spiritual presence, an ever-dominant personality. I could almost fancy that I saw him standing in the shadow of my room, so well had Shakespeare drawn him, with his golden hair, his tender flower-like grace, his dreamy deep-sunken eyes, his delicate mobile limbs, and his white lily hands. His very name fascinated me. Willie Hughes! Willie Hughes! How musically it sounded! Yes: who else but he could have been the master-mistress of Shakespeare's passion, the lord of his love to whom he was bound in vassalage, the delicate minion of pleasure, the rose of the whole world, the herald of the spring decked in the proud livery of youth, the lovely boy whom it was sweet music to hear, and whose beauty was the very raiment of Shakespeare's heart, as it was the keystone of his dramatic power? How bitter now seemed the whole tragedy of his desertion and his shame! — shame that he made sweet and lovely by the mere magic of his personality, but that was none the less shame. Yet as Shakespeare forgave him, should not we forgive him also? I did not care to pry into the mystery of his sin.

His abandonment of Shakespeare's theatre was a different matter, and I investigated it at great length. Finally I came to the conclusion that Cyril Graham had been wrong in regarding the rival dramatist of the 80th Sonnet as Chapman. It was obviously Marlowe who was alluded to. At the time the Sonnets were written, such an expression as 'the proud full sail of his great verse' could not have been used of Chapman's work, however applicable it might have been to the style of his later Jacobean plays. No: Marlowe was clearly the rival dramatist of whom Shakespeare spoke in such laudatory terms; and that

> Affable familiar ghost
> Which nightly gulls him with intelligence

was the Mephistopheles of his Doctor Faustus. No doubt, Marlowe was fascinated by the beauty and grace of the boy-actor, and lured him away from the Blackfriars' Theatre, that he might play the Gaveston of his *Edward II*. That Shakespeare had the legal right to retain Willie Hughes in his own company is evident from Sonnet LXXXVII, where he says: —

Farewell! thou are too dear for my possessing,
And like enough thou know'st thy estimate:
The *charter of thy worth* gives thee releasing:
My *bonds* in thee are all determinate.
For how do I hold thee but by thy granting?
And for that riches where is my deserving?
The cause of this fair gift in me is wanting,
And so my patent back again is swerving.
Thyself thou gavest, thy own work then not knowing,
Or me, to whom thou gavest it, else mistaking;
So thy great gift, upon misprision growing,
Comes home again, on better judgment making.
    Thus have I had thee, as a dream doth flatter,
    In sleep a king, but waking no such matter.

But him whom he could not hold by love, he would not hold by force. Willie Hughes became a member of Lord Pembroke's company, and, perhaps in the open yard of the Red Bull Tavern, played the part of King Edward's delicate minion. On Marlowe's death, he seems to have returned to Shakespeare, who, whatever his fellow-partners may have thought of the matter, was not slow to forgive the wilfulness and treachery of the young actor.

How well, too, had Shakespeare drawn the temperament of the stage-player! Willie Hughes was one of those

> That do not do the thing they most do show,
> Who, moving others, are themselves as stone.

He could act love, but could not feel it, could mimic passion without realizing it.

> In many's looks the false heart's history
> Is writ in moods and frowns and wrinkles strange,

but with Willie Hughes it was not so. 'Heaven,' says Shakespeare, in a sonnet of mad idolatry —

> Heaven in thy creation did decree
> That in thy face sweet love should ever dwell;
> Whate'er thy thoughts or thy heart's workings be,
> Thy looks should nothing thence but sweetness tell.

In his 'inconstant mind' and his 'false heart', it was easy to recognize the insincerity and treachery that somehow seem inseparable from the artistic nature, as in his love of praise, that desire for immediate recognition that characterizes all actors. And yet, more fortunate in this than other actors, Willie Hughes was to know something of immortality. Inseparably connected with Shakespeare's plays, he was to live in them.

> Your name from hence immortal life shall have,
> Though I, once gone, to all the world must die:
> The earth can yield me but a common grave,
> When you entombed in men's eyes shall lie.
> Your monument shall be my gentle verse,
> Which eyes not yet created shall o'er-read,
> And tongues to be your being shall rehearse
> When all the breathers of this world are dead.

There were endless allusions, also, to Willie Hughes's power over his audience, – the 'gazers,' as Shakespeare calls them; but perhaps the most perfect description of his wonderful mastery over dramatic art was in *The Lover's Complaint*, where Shakespeare says of him: –

> In him a plenitude of subtle matter,
> Applied to cautels, all strange forms receives,
> Of burning blushes, or of weeping water,
> Or swooning paleness; and he takes and leaves.

In either's aptness, as it best deceives,
To blush at speeches rank, to weep at woes,
Or to turn white and swoon at tragic shows.

So on the tip of his subduing tongue,
All kinds of arguments and questions deep,
All replication prompt and reason strong,
For his advantage still did wake and sleep.
To make the weeper laugh, the laugher weep,
He had the dialect and the different skill,
Catching all passions in his craft of will.

Once I thought that I had really found Willie
Hughes in Elizabethan literature. In a wonderfully
graphic account of the last days of the great Earl of
Essex, his chaplain, Thomas Knell, tells us that the
night before the Earl died, 'he called William
Hewes, which was his musician, to play upon the
virginals and to sing. "Play," said he, "my song,
Will Hewes, and I will sing it myself." So he did it
most joyfully, not as the howling swan, which, still
looking down, waileth her end, but as a sweet lark,
lifting up his hands and casting up his eyes to his
God, with this mounted the crystal skies, and
reached with his unwearied tongue the top of
highest heavens.' Surely the boy who played on the

virginals to the dying father of Sidney's Stella was none other but the Will Hews to whom Shakespeare dedicated the Sonnets, and whom he tells us was himself sweet 'music to hear'. Yet Lord Essex died in 1576, when Shakespeare himself was but twelve years of age. It was impossible that his musician could have been the Mr W. H. of the Sonnets. Perhaps Shakespeare's young friend was the son of the player upon the virginals? It was at least something to have discovered that Will Hews was an Elizabethan name. Indeed the name Hews seemed to have been closely connected with music and the stage. The first English actress was the lovely Margaret Hews, whom Prince Rupert so madly loved. What more probable than that between her and Lord Essex's musician had come the boy-actor of Shakespeare's plays? But the proofs, the links — where were they? Alas! I could not find them. It seemed to me that I was always on the brink of absolute verification, but that I could never really attain to it.

From Willie Hughes's life I soon passed to thoughts of his death. I used to wonder what had been his end.

Perhaps he had been one of those English actors who in 1604 went across sea to Germany and played before the great Duke Henry Julius of Brunswick, himself a dramatist of no mean order, and at the Court of that strange Elector of Brandenburg, who was so enamoured of beauty that he was said to have bought for his weight in amber the young son of a travelling Greek merchant, and to have given pageants in honour of his slave all through that dreadful famine year of 1606–7, when the people died of hunger in the very streets of the town, and for the space of seven months there was no rain. We know at any rate that *Romeo and Juliet* was brought out at Dresden in 1613, along with *Hamlet* and *King Lear*, and it was surely to none other than Willie Hughes that in 1615 the death-mask of Shakespeare was brought by the hand of one of the suite of the English ambassador, pale token of the passing away of the great poet who had so dearly loved him. Indeed there would have been something peculiarly fitting in the idea that the boy-actor, whose beauty had been so vital an element in the realism and romance of Shakespeare's art, should

47

have been the first to have brought to Germany the seed of the new culture, and was in his way the precursor of that *Aufklarung* or Illumination of the eighteenth century, that splendid movement which, though begun by Lessing and Herder, and brought to its full and perfect issue by Goethe, was in no small part helped on by another actor – Friedrich Schroeder – who awoke the popular consciousness, and by means of the feigned passions and mimetic methods of the stage showed the intimate, the vital, connection between life and literature. If this was so, – and there was certainly no evidence against it, – it was not improbable that Willie Hughes was one of those English comedians (*mimae quidam ex Britannia*, as the old chronicle calls them), who were slain at Nuremberg in a sudden uprising of the people, and were secretly buried in a little vineyard outside the city by some young men 'who had found pleasure in their performances, and of whom some had sought to be instructed in the mysteries of the new art'. Certainly no more fitting place could there be for him to whom Shakespeare said, 'thou art all my art,' than this little vineyard outside the city walls. For was it not from the sorrows of Dionysos that Tragedy sprang? Was not the light laughter of Comedy, with its careless merriment and quick replies, first heard on the lips of the Sicilian vine-dressers? Nay, did not the purple and red satin of the wine-froth on face and limbs give the first suggestion of the charm and fascination of disguise – the desire for self-concealment, the sense of the value of objectivity thus showing itself in the rude beginnings of the art? At any rate, wherever he lay – whether in the little vineyard at the gate of the Gothic town, or in some dim London churchyard amidst the roar and bustle of our great city – no gorgeous monument marked his resting-place. His true tomb, as Shakespeare saw, was the poet's verse, his true monument the permanence of the drama. So had it been with others whose beauty had given a new creative impulse to their age. The ivory body of the Bithynian slave rots in the green ooze of the Nile, and on the yellow hills of the Cerameicus is strewn the dust of the young Athenian; but Antinous lives in sculpture, and Charmides in philosophy.

•

After three weeks had elapsed, I determined to make a strong appeal to Erskine to do justice to the memory of Cyril Graham, and to give to the world his marvellous interpretation of the Sonnets – the only interpretation that thoroughly explained the problem. I have not any copy of my letter, I regret to say, nor have I been able to lay my hand upon the original; but I remember that I went over the whole ground, and covered sheets of paper with passionate reiteration of the arguments and proofs that my study had suggested to me. It seemed to me that I was not merely restoring Cyril Graham to his proper place in literary history, but rescuing the honour of Shakespeare himself from the tedious memory of a commonplace intrigue. I put into the letter all my enthusiasm. I put into the letter all my faith.

No sooner, in fact, had I sent it off than a curious reaction came over me. It seemed to me that I had given away my capacity for belief in the Willie Hughes theory of the Sonnets, that something had gone out of me, as it were, and that I was perfectly indifferent to the whole subject. What was it that had happened? It is difficult to say. Perhaps, by finding perfect expression for a passion, I had exhausted the passion itself. Emotional forces, like the forces of physical life, have their positive limitations. Perhaps the mere effort to convert any one to a theory involves some form of renunciation of the power of credence. Perhaps I was simply tired of the whole thing, and my enthusiasm having burnt out, my reason was left to its own unimpassioned judgment. However it came about, and I cannot pretend to explain it, there was no doubt that Willie Hughes suddenly became to me a mere myth, an idle dream, the boyish fancy of a young man who, like most ardent spirits, was more anxious to convince others than to be himself convinced.

As I had said some very unjust and bitter things to Erskine in my letter, I determined to go and see him at once, and to make my apologies to him for my behaviour. Accordingly, the next morning I drove down to Birdcage Walk, and found Erskine sitting in his library, with the forged picture of Willie Hughes in front of him.

'My dear Erskine!' I cried, 'I have come to apologize to you.'

'To apologize to me?' he said. 'What for?'

'For my letter,' I answered.

'You have nothing to regret in your letter,' he said. 'On the contrary, you have done me the greatest service in your power. You have shown me that Cyril Graham's theory is perfectly sound.'

'You don't mean to say that you believe in Willie Hughes?' I exclaimed.

'Why not?' he rejoined. 'You have proved the thing to me. Do you think I cannot estimate the value of evidence?'

'But there is no evidence at all,' I groaned, sinking into a chair. 'When I wrote to you I was under the influence of a perfectly silly enthusiasm. I had been touched by the story of Cyril Graham's death, fascinated by his romantic theory, enthralled by the wonder and novelty of the whole idea. I see now that the theory is based on a delusion. The only evidence for the existence of Willie Hughes is that picture in front of you, and the picture is a forgery. Don't be carried away by mere sentiment in this matter. Whatever romance may have to say about the Willie Hughes theory, reason is dead against it.'

'I don't understand you,' said Erskine, looking at me in amazement. 'Why, you yourself have convinced me by your letter that Willie Hughes is an absolute reality. Why have you changed your mind? Or is all that you have been saying to me merely a joke?'

'I cannot explain it to you,' I rejoined, 'but I see now that there is really nothing to be said in favour of Cyril Graham's interpretation. The Sonnets are addressed to Lord Pembroke. For heaven's sake don't waste your time in a foolish attempt to discover a young Elizabethan actor who never existed, and to make a phantom puppet the centre of the great cycle of Shakespeare's Sonnets.'

'I see that you don't understand the theory,' he replied.

'My dear Erskine,' I cried, 'not understand it! Why, I feel as if I had invented it. Surely my letter shows you that I not merely went into the whole matter, but that I contributed proofs of every kind. The one flaw in the theory is that it presupposes the existence of the person whose existence is the subject of dispute. If we grant that there was in Shakespeare's company a young actor of the name of Willie Hughes, it is not difficult to make him the object of the Sonnets. But as we know that there was no actor of this name in the company of the Globe Theatre, it is idle to pursue the investigation further.'

'But that is exactly what we don't know,' said Erskine. 'It is quite true that his name does not occur in the list given in the first folio; but, as Cyril pointed out, that is rather a proof in favour of the existence of Willie Hughes than against it, if we remember his treacherous desertion of Shakespeare for a rival dramatist.'

We argued the matter over for hours, but nothing that I could say could make Erskine surrender his faith in Cyril Graham's interpretation. He told me that he intended to devote his life to proving the theory, and that he was determined to do justice to Cyril Graham's memory. I entreated him, laughed at him, begged of him, but it was of no use. Finally we parted, not exactly in anger, but certainly with a shadow between us. He thought me shallow, I thought him foolish. When I called on him again, his servant told me that he had gone to Germany.

Two years afterwards, as I was going into my club, the hall-porter handed me a letter with a foreign postmark. It was from Erskine, and written at the Hotel d'Angleterre, Cannes. When I had read it I was filled with horror, though I did not quite believe that he would be so mad as to carry his resolve into execution. The gist of the letter was that he had tried in every way to verify the Willie Hughes theory, and had failed, and that as Cyril Graham had given his life for this theory, he himself had determined to give his own life also to the same cause. The concluding words of the letter were these: 'I still believe in Willie Hughes; and by the time you receive this, I shall have died by my own hand for Willie Hughes's sake: for his sake, and for the sake of Cyril Graham, whom I drove to his death by my shallow scepticism and ignorant lack of faith. The truth was once revealed to you, and you rejected it. It comes to you now stained with the blood of two lives, – do not turn away from it.'

It was a horrible moment. I felt sick with misery, and yet I could not believe it. To die for one's theological beliefs is the worst use a man can make of his life, but to die for a literary theory! It seemed impossible.

I looked at the date. The letter was a week old. Some unfortunate chance had prevented my going to the club for several days, or I might have got it in time to save him. Perhaps it was not too late. I drove off to my rooms, packed up my things, and started by the night-mail from Charing Cross. The journey was intolerable. I thought I would never arrive. As soon as I did I drove to the Hotel d'Angleterre. They told me that Erskine had been buried two days before, in the English cemetery. There was something horribly grotesque about the whole tragedy. I said all kinds of wild things, and the people in the hall looked curiously at me.

Suddenly Lady Erskine, in deep mourning, passed across the vestibule. When she saw me she came up to me, murmured something about her poor son, and burst into tears. I led her into her sitting-room. An elderly gentleman was there waiting for her. It was the English doctor.

We talked a great deal about Erskine, but I said nothing about his motive for committing suicide. It was evident that he had not told his mother anything about the reason that had driven him to so fatal, so mad an act. Finally Lady Erskine rose and said, 'George left you something as a memento. It was a thing he prized very much. I will get it for you.'

As soon as she had left the room I turned to the doctor and said, 'What a dreadful shock it must have been to Lady Erskine! I wonder that she bears it as well as she does.'

'Oh, she knew for months past that it was coming,' he answered.

'Knew it for months past!' I cried. 'But why didn't she stop him? Why didn't she have him watched? He must have been mad.'

The doctor stared at me. 'I don't know what you mean,' he said.

'Well,' I cried, 'if a mother knows that her son is going to commit suicide –'

'Suicide!' he answered. 'Poor Erskine did not commit suicide. He died of consumption. He came here to die. The moment I saw him I knew that there was no hope. One lung was almost gone, and the other was very much affected. Three days before he died he asked me was there any hope. I told him frankly that there was none, and that he had only a few days to live. He wrote some letters, and was quite resigned, retaining his senses to the last.'

At that moment Lady Erskine entered the room with the fatal picture of Willie Hughes in her hand. 'When George was dying he begged me to give you this,' she said. As I took it from her, her tears fell on my hand.

The picture hangs now in my library, where it is very much admired by my artistic friends. They have decided that it is not a Clouet, but an Ouvry. I have never cared to tell them its true history. But sometimes when I look at it, I think that there is really a great deal to be said for the Willie Hughes theory of Shakespeare's Sonnets.

The Ballad of Reading Gaol

In memoriam C.T.W.
sometime trooper of the Royal Horse Guards
obiit H.M. prison, Reading, Berkshire, July 7, 1896

I

He did not wear his scarlet coat,
   For blood and wine are red,
And blood and wine were on his hands
   When they found him with the dead,
The poor dead woman whom he loved,
   And murdered in her bed.

He walked amongst the Trial Men
   In a suit of shabby grey;
A cricket cap was on his head,
   And his step seemed light and gay;
But I never saw a man who looked
   So wistfully at the day.

I never saw a man who looked
   With such a wistful eye

Upon that little tent of blue
    Which prisoners call the sky,
And at every drifting cloud that went
    With sails of silver by.

I walked, with other souls in pain,
    Within another ring,
And was wondering if the man had done
    A great or little thing,
When a voice behind me whispered low,
    'That fellow's got to swing.'

Dear Christ! the very prison walls
    Suddenly seemed to reel,
And the sky above my head became
    Like a casque of scorching steel;
And, though I was a soul in pain,
    My pain I could not feel.

I only knew what hunted thought
    Quickened his step, and why
He looked upon the garish day
    With such a wistful eye;
The man had killed the thing he loved,
    And so he had to die.

•

Yet each man kills the thing he loves,
By each let this be heard,
Some do it with a bitter look,
Some with a flattering word,
The coward does it with a kiss,
The brave man with a sword!

Some kill their love when they are young,
And some when they are old;
Some strangle with the hands of Lust,
Some with the hands of Gold:
The kindest use a knife, because
The dead so soon grow cold.

Some love too little, some too long,
Some sell, and others buy;
Some do the deed with many tears,
And some without a sigh:
For each man kills the thing he loves,
Yet each man does not die.

He does not die a death of shame
On a day of dark disgrace,
Nor have a noose about his neck,
Nor a cloth upon his face,
Nor drop feet foremost through the floor
Into an empty space.

He does not sit with silent men
    Who watch him night and day;
Who watch him when he tries to weep,
    And when he tries to pray;
Who watch him lest himself should rob
    The prison of its prey.

He does not wake at dawn to see
    Dread figures throng his room,
The shivering Chaplain robed in white,
    The Sheriff stern with gloom,
And the Governor all in shiny black,
    With the yellow face of Doom.

He does not rise in piteous haste
    To put on convict-clothes,
While some coarse-mouthed Doctor
        gloats, and notes
    Each new and nerve-twitched pose,
Fingering a watch whose little ticks
    Are like horrible hammer-blows.

He does not feel that sickening thirst
    That sands one's throat, before
The hangman with his gardener's gloves
    Comes through the padded door,
And binds one with three leathern thongs,
    That the throat may thirst no more.

He does not bend his head to hear
    The Burial Office read,
Nor, while the anguish of his soul
    Tells him he is not dead,
Cross his own coffin, as he moves
    Into the hideous shed.

He does not stare upon the air
    Through a little roof of glass:
He does not pray with lips of clay
    For his agony to pass;
Nor feel upon his shuddering cheek
    The kiss of Caiaphas.

II

Six weeks the guardsman walked the yard
    In the suit of shabby grey:
His cricket cap was on his head,
    And his step seemed light and gay,
But I never saw a man who looked
    So wistfully at the day.

I never saw a man who looked
    With such a wistful eye
Upon that little tent of blue
    Which prisoners call the sky,

And at every wandering cloud that trailed
　Its ravelled fleeces by.

He did not wring his hands, as do
　Those witless men who dare
To try to rear the changeling Hope
　In the cave of black Despair:
He only looked upon the sun,
　And drank the morning air.

He did not wring his hands nor weep,
　Nor did he peek or pine,
But he drank the air as though it held
　Some healthful anodyne;
With open mouth he drank the sun
　As though it had been wine!

And I and all the souls in pain,
　Who tramped the other ring,
Forgot if we ourselves had done
　A great or little thing,
And watched with gaze of dull amaze
　The man who had to swing.

For strange it was to see him pass
　With a step so light and gay,
And strange it was to see him look
　So wistfully at the day,

And strange it was to think that he
    Had such a debt to pay.

            •

For oak and elm have pleasant leaves
    That in the spring-time shoot:
But grim to see is the gallows-tree,
    With its adder-bitten root,
And, green or dry, a man must die
    Before it bears its fruit!

The loftiest place is that seat of grace
    For which all worldlings try:
But who would stand in hempen band
    Upon a scaffold high,
And through a murderer's collar take
    His last look at the sky?

It is sweet to dance to violins
    When Love and Life are fair:
To dance to flutes, to dance to lutes
    Is delicate and rare:
But it is not sweet with nimble feet
    To dance upon the air!

So with curious eye and sick surmise
    We watched him day by day,

And wondered if each one of us
    Would end the self-same way,
For none can tell to what red Hell
    His sightless soul may stray.

At last the dead man walked no more
    Amongst the Trial Men,
And I knew that he was standing up
    In the black dock's dreadful pen,
And that never would I see his face
    For weal or woe again.

Like two doomed ships that pass in storm
    We had crossed each other's way:
But we made no sign, we said no word,
    We had no word to say;
For we did not meet in the holy night,
    But in the shameful day.

A prison wall was round us both,
    Two outcast men we were:
The world had thrust us from its heart,
    And God from out His care:
And the iron gin that waits for Sin
    Had caught us in its snare.

III

In Debtors' Yard the stones are hard,
  And the dripping wall is high,
So it was there he took his air
  Beneath the leaden sky,
And by each side a warder walked,
  For fear the man might die.

Or else he sat with those who watched
  His anguish night and day;
Who watched him when he rose to weep,
  And when he crouched to pray;
Who watched him lest himself should rob
  Their scaffold of its prey.

The Governor was strong upon
  The Regulations Act:
The Doctor said that Death was but
  A scientific fact:
And twice a day the Chaplain called,
  And left a little tract.

And twice a day he smoked his pipe,
  And drank his quart of beer:
His soul was resolute, and held
  No hiding-place for fear;

He often said that he was glad
   The hangman's day was near.

But why he said so strange a thing
   No warder dared to ask:
For he to whom a watcher's doom
   Is given as his task,
Must set a lock upon his lips
   And make his face a mask.

Or else he might be moved, and try
   To comfort or console:
And what should Human Pity do
   Pent up in Murderer's Hole?
What word of grace in such a place
   Could help a brother's soul?

With slouch and swing around the ring
   We trod the Fools' Parade!
We did not care: we knew we were
   The Devil's Own Brigade:
And shaven head and feet of lead
   Make a merry masquerade.

We tore the tarry rope to shreds
   With blunt and bleeding nails;
We rubbed the doors, and scrubbed the floors,
   And cleaned the shining rails:

And, rank by rank, we soaped the plank,
  And clattered with the pails.

We sewed the sacks, we broke the stones,
  We turned the dusty drill:
We banged the tins, and bawled the hymns,
  And sweated on the mill:
But in the heart of every man
  Terror was lying still.

So still it lay that every day
  Crawled like a weed-clogged wave:
And we forgot the bitter lot
  That waits for fool and knave,
Till once, as we tramped in from work,
  We passed an open grave.

With yawning mouth the yellow hole
  Gaped for a living thing;
The very mud cried out for blood
  To the thirsty asphalt ring;
And we knew that ere one dawn grew fair
  Some prisoner had to swing.

Right in we went, with soul intent
  On Death and Dread and Doom:
The hangman, with his little bag,
  Went shuffling through the gloom:

And I trembled as I groped my way
 Into my numbered tomb.

·

That night the empty corridors
 Were full of forms of Fear,
And up and down the iron town
 Stole feet we could not hear,
And through the bars that hide the stars
 White faces seemed to peer.

He lay as one who lies and dreams
 In a pleasant meadow-land,
The watchers watched him as he slept,
 And could not understand
How one could sleep so sweet a sleep
 With a hangman close at hand.

But there is no sleep when men must weep
 Who never yet have wept:
So we – the fool, the fraud, the knave –
 That endless vigil kept,
And through each brain on hands of pain
 Another's terror crept.

Alas! it is a fearful thing
 To feel another's guilt!

For, right, within, the Sword of Sin
    Pierced to its poisoned hilt,
And as molten lead were the tears we shed
    For the blood we had not spilt.

The warders with their shoes of felt
    Crept by each padlocked door,
And peeped and saw, with eyes of awe,
    Grey figures on the floor,
And wondered why men knelt to pray
    Who never prayed before.

All through the night we knelt and prayed,
    Mad mourners of a corse!
The troubled plumes of midnight shook
    The plume upon a hearse:
The bitter wine upon a sponge
    Was the savour of Remorse.

•

The grey cock crew, the red cock crew,
    But never came the day:
And crooked shapes of Terror crouched,
    In the corners where we lay:
And each evil sprite that walks by night
    Before us seemed to play.

They glided past, they glided fast,
    Like travellers through a mist:
They mocked the moon in a rigadoon
    Of delicate turn and twist,
And with formal pace and loathsome grace
    The phantoms kept their tryst.

With mop and mow, we saw them go,
    Slim shadows hand in hand:
About, about, in ghostly rout
    They trod a saraband:
And the damned grotesques made arabesque
    Like the wind upon the sand!

With the pirouettes of marionettes,
    They tripped on pointed tread:
But with flutes of Fear they filled the ear,
    As their grisly masque they led,
And loud they sang, and long they sang,
    For they sang to wake the dead.

'Oho!' they cried. 'The world is wide,
    But fettered limbs go lame!
And once, or twice, to throw the dice
    Is a gentlemanly game,
But he does not win who plays with Sin
    In the secret House of Shame.'

No things of air these antics were,
  That frolicked with such glee:
To men whose lives were held in gyves,
  And whose feet might not go free,
Ah! wounds of Christ! they were living things,
  Most terrible to see.

Around, around, they waltzed and wound;
  Some wheeled in smirking pairs;
With the mincing step of a demirep
  Some sidled up the stairs;
And with subtle sneer, and fawning leer,
  Each helped us at our prayers.

The morning wind began to moan,
  But still the night went on:
Through its giant loom the web of gloom
  Crept till each thread was spun:
And, as we prayed, we grew afraid
  Of the Justice of the Sun.

The moaning wind went wandering round
  The weeping prison-wall:
Till like a wheel of turning steel
  We felt the minutes crawl:
O moaning wind! what had we done
  To have such a seneschal?

73

At last I saw the shadowed bars,
    Like a lattice wrought in lead,
Move right across the whitewashed wall
    That faced my three-plank bed,
And I knew that somewhere in the world
    God's dreadful dawn was red.

At six o'clock we cleaned our cells,
    At seven all was still,
But the sough and swing of a mighty wing
    The prison seemed to fill,
For the Lord of Death with icy breath
    Had entered in to kill.

He did not pass in purple pomp,
    Nor ride a moon-white steed.
Three yards of cord and a sliding board
    Are all the gallows' need:
So with rope of shame the Herald came
    To do the secret deed.

We were as men who through a fen
    Of filthy darkness grope:
We did not dare to breathe a prayer,
    Or to give our anguish scope:
Something was dead in each of us,
    And what was dead was Hope.

For Man's grim Justice goes its way,
    And will not swerve aside:
It slays the weak, it slays the strong,
    It has a deadly stride:
With iron heel it slays the strong,
    The monstrous parricide!

We waited for the stroke of eight:
    Each tongue was thick with thirst:
For the stroke of eight is the stroke of Fate
    That makes a man accursed,
And Fate will use a running noose
    For the best man and the worst.

We had no other thing to do,
    Save to wait for the sign to come:
So, like things of stone in a valley lone,
    Quiet we sat and dumb:
But each man's heart beat thick and quick,
    Like a madman on a drum!

With sudden shock the prison-clock
    Smote on the shivering air,
And from all the gaol rose up a wail
    Of impotent despair,
Like the sound that frightened marshes hear
    From some leper in his lair.

And as one sees most fearful things
  In the crystal of a dream,
We saw the greasy hempen rope
  Hooked to the blackened beam,
And heard the prayer the hangman's snare
  Strangled into a scream.

And all the woe that moved him so
  That he gave that bitter cry,
And the wild regrets, and the bloody sweats,
  None knew so well as I:
For he who lives more lives than one
  More deaths than one must die.

IV

There is no chapel on the day
  On which they hang a man:
The Chaplain's heart is far too sick,
  Or his face is far too wan,
Or there is that written in his eyes
  Which none should look upon.

So they kept us close till nigh on noon,
  And then they rang the bell,

And the warders with their jingling keys
    Opened each listening cell,
And down the iron stair we tramped,
    Each from his separate Hell.

Out into God's sweet air we went,
    But not in wonted way,
For this man's face was white with fear,
    And that man's face was grey,
And I never saw sad men who looked
    So wistfully at the day.

I never saw sad men who looked
    With such a wistful eye
Upon that little tent of blue
    We prisoners called the sky,
And at every happy cloud that passed
    In such strange freedom by.

But there were those amongst us all
    Who walked with downcast head,
And knew that, had each got his due,
    They should have died instead:
He had but killed a thing that lived,
    Whilst they had killed the dead.

For he who sins a second time
    Wakes a dead soul to pain,

And draws it from its spotted shroud,
　　And makes it bleed again,
And makes it bleed great gouts of blood,
　　And makes it bleed in vain!

·

Like ape or clown, in monstrous garb
　　With crooked arrows starred,
Silently we went round and round
　　The slippery asphalt yard;
Silently we went round and round,
　　And no man spoke a word.

Silently we went round and round,
　　And through each hollow mind
The Memory of dreadful things
　　Rushed like a dreadful wind,
And Horror stalked before each man,
　　And Terror crept behind.

·

The warders strutted up and down,
　　And watched their herd of brutes,
Their uniforms were spick and span,
　　And they wore their Sunday suits,

But we knew the work they had been at
   By the quicklime on their boots.

For where a grave had opened wide,
   There was no grave at all:
Only a stretch of mud and sand
   By the hideous prison-wall,
And a little heap of burning lime,
   That the man should have his pall.

For he has a pall, this wretched man,
   Such as few men can claim:
Deep down below a prison-yard,
   Naked for greater shame,
He lies, with fetters on each foot,
   Wrapt in a sheet of flame!

And all the while the burning lime
   Eats flesh and bone away,
It eats the brittle bone by night,
   And the soft flesh by day,
It eats the flesh and bone by turns,
   But it eats the heart alway.

•

For three long years they will not sow
   Or root or seedling there:

For three long years the unblessed spot
    Will sterile be and bare,
And look upon the wondering sky
    With unreproachful stare.

They think a murderer's heart would taint
    Each simple seed they sow.
It is not true! God's kindly earth
    Is kindlier than men know,
And the red rose would but blow more red,
    The white rose whiter blow.

Out of his mouth a red, red rose!
    Out of his heart a white!
For who can say by what strange way,
    Christ brings His will to light,
Since the barren staff the pilgrim bore
    Bloomed in the great Pope's sight?

But neither milk-white rose nor red
    May bloom in prison-air;
The shard, the pebble, and the flint,
    Are what they give us there:
For flowers have been known to heal
    A common man's despair.

So never will wine-red rose or white,
    Petal by petal, fall

On that stretch of mud and sand that lies
  By the hideous prison-wall,
To tell the men who tramp the yard
  That God's Son died for all.

．

Yet though the hideous prison-wall
  Still hems him round and round,
And a spirit may not walk by night
  That is with fetters bound,
And a spirit may but weep that lies
  In such unholy ground.

He is at peace – this wretched man —
  At peace, or will be soon:
There is no thing to make him mad,
  Nor does Terror walk at noon,
For the lampless Earth in which he lies
  Has neither Sun nor Moon.

They hanged him as a beast is hanged:
  They did not even toll
A requiem that might have brought
  Rest to his startled soul,
But hurriedly they took him out,
  And hid him in a hole.

The warders stripped him of his clothes,
    And gave him to the flies:
They mocked the swollen purple throat,
    And the stark and staring eyes:
And with laughter loud they heaped the shroud
    In which the convict lies.

The Chaplain would not kneel to pray
    By his dishonoured grave:
Nor mark it with that blessed Cross
    That Christ for sinners gave,
Because the man was one of those
    Whom Christ came down to save.

Yet all is well; he has but passed
    To Life's appointed bourne:
And alien tears will fill for him
    Pity's long-broken urn,
For his mourners will be outcast men,
    And outcasts always mourn.

V

I know not whether Laws be right,
    Or whether Laws be wrong;

All that we know who lie in gaol
    Is that the wall is strong;
And that each day is like a year,
    A year whose days are long.

But this I know, that every Law
    That men have made for Man,
Since first Man took his brother's life,
    And the sad world began,
But straws the wheat and saves the chaff
    With a most evil fan.

This too I know – and wise it were
    If each could know the same –
That every prison that men build
    Is built with bricks of shame,
And bound with bars lest Christ should see
    How men their brothers maim.

With bars they blur the gracious moon,
    And blind the goodly sun:
And they do well to hide their Hell,
    For in it things are done
That Son of God nor son of Man
    Ever should look upon!

•

The vilest deeds like poison weeds,
    Bloom well in prison-air;
It is only what is good in Man
    That wastes and withers there:
Pale Anguish keeps the heavy gate,
    And the Warder is Despair.

For they starve the little frightened child
    Till it weeps both night and day:
And they scourge the weak, and flog the fool,
    And gibe the old and grey,
And some grow mad, and all grow bad,
    And none a word may say.

Each narrow cell in which we dwell
    Is a foul and dark latrine,
And the fetid breath of living Death
    Chokes up each grated screen,
And all, but Lust, is turned to dust
    In humanity's machine.

The brackish water that we drink
    Creeps with a loathsome slime,
And the bitter bread they weigh in scales
    Is full of chalk and lime,
And Sleep will not lie down, but walks
    Wild-eyed, and cries to Time.

•

But though lean Hunger and green Thirst
  Like asp with adder fight,
We have little care of prison fare,
  For what chills and kills outright
Is that every stone one lifts by day
  Becomes one's heart by night.

With midnight always in one's heart,
  And twilight in one's cell,
We turn the crank, or tear the rope,
  Each in his separate Hell,
And the silence is more awful far
  Than the sound of a brazen bell.

And never a human voice comes near
  To speak a gentle word:
And the eye that watches through the door
  Is pitiless and hard:
And by all forgot, we rot and rot,
  With soul and body marred.

And thus we rust Life's iron chain
  Degraded and alone:
And some men curse, and some men weep,
  And some men make no moan:
But God's eternal Laws are kind
  And break the heart of stone.

And every human heart that breaks,
  In prison-cell or yard,
Is as that broken box that gave
  Its treasure to the Lord,
And filled the unclean leper's house
  With the scent of costliest nard.

Ah! happy they whose hearts can break
  And peace of pardon win!
How else may man make straight his plan
  And cleanse his soul from Sin!
How else but through a broken heart
  May Lord Christ enter in?

.

And he of the swollen purple throat,
  And the stark and staring eyes,
Waits for the holy hands that took
  The thief to Paradise;
And a broken and a contrite heart
  The Lord will not despise.

The man in red who reads the Law
  Gave him three weeks of life,
Three little weeks in which to heal
  His soul of his soul's strife,

And cleanse from every blot of blood
   The hand that held the knife.

And with tears of blood he cleansed the hand,
   The hand that held the steel:
For only blood can wipe out blood,
   And only tears can heal:
And the crimson srain that was of Cain
   Became Christ's snow-white seal.

VI

In Reading gaol by Reading town
   There is a pit of shame,
And in it lies a wretched man
   Eaten by teeth of flame,
In a burning winding-sheet he lies,
   And his grave has got no name.

And there, till Christ call forth the dead,
   In silence let him lie:
No need to waste the foolish tear,
   Or heave the windy sigh:
The man had killed the thing he loved,
   And so he had to die.

And all men kill the thing they love,
    By all let this be heard,
Some do it with a bitter look,
    Some with a flattering word,
The coward does it with a kiss,
    The brave man with a sword!

PENGUIN 60s CLASSICS

APOLLONIUS OF RHODES · *Jason and the Argonauts*
ARISTOPHANES · *Lysistrata*
SAINT AUGUSTINE · *Confessions of a Sinner*
JANE AUSTEN · *The History of England*
HONORÉ DE BALZAC · *The Atheist's Mass*
BASHŌ · *Haiku*
GIOVANNI BOCCACCIO · *Ten Tales from the* Decameron
JAMES BOSWELL · *Meeting Dr Johnson*
CHARLOTTE BRONTË · *Mina Laury*
CAO XUEQIN · *The Dream of the Red Chamber*
THOMAS CARLYLE · *On Great Men*
BALDESAR CASTIGLIONE · *Etiquette for Renaissance Gentlemen*
CERVANTES · *The Jealous Extremaduran*
KATE CHOPIN · *The Kiss*
JOSEPH CONRAD · *The Secret Sharer*
DANTE · *The First Three Circles of Hell*
CHARLES DARWIN · *The Galapagos Islands*
THOMAS DE QUINCEY · *The Pleasures and Pains of Opium*
DANIEL DEFOE · *A Visitation of the Plague*
BERNAL DÍAZ · *The Betrayal of Montezuma*
FYODOR DOSTOYEVSKY · *The Gentle Spirit*
FREDERICK DOUGLASS · *The Education of Frederick Douglass*
GEORGE ELIOT · *The Lifted Veil*
GUSTAVE FLAUBERT · *A Simple Heart*
BENJAMIN FRANKLIN · *The Means and Manner of Obtaining Virtue*
EDWARD GIBBON · *Reflections on the Fall of Rome*
CHARLOTTE PERKINS GILMAN · *The Yellow Wallpaper*
GOETHE · *Letters from Italy*
HOMER · *The Rage of Achilles*
HOMER · *The Voyages of Odysseus*

PENGUIN 60s CLASSICS

HENRY JAMES · *The Lesson of the Master*
FRANZ KAFKA · *The Judgement*
THOMAS À KEMPIS · *Counsels on the Spiritual Life*
HEINRICH VON KLEIST · *The Marquise of O—*
LIVY · *Hannibal's Crossing of the Alps*
NICCOLÒ MACHIAVELLI · *The Art of War*
SIR THOMAS MALORY · *The Death of King Arthur*
GUY DE MAUPASSANT · *Boule de Suif*
FRIEDRICH NIETZSCHE · *Zarathustra's Discourses*
OVID · *Orpheus in the Underworld*
PLATO · *Phaedrus*
EDGAR ALLAN POE · *The Murders in the Rue Morgue*
ARTHUR RIMBAUD · *A Season in Hell*
JEAN-JACQUES ROUSSEAU · *Meditations of a Solitary Walker*
ROBERT LOUIS STEVENSON · *Dr Jekyll and Mr Hyde*
TACITUS · *Nero and the Burning of Rome*
HENRY DAVID THOREAU · *Civil Disobedience*
LEO TOLSTOY · *The Death of Ivan Ilyich*
IVAN TURGENEV · *Three Sketches from a Hunter's Album*
MARK TWAIN · *The Man That Corrupted Hadleyburg*
GIORGIO VASARI · *Lives of Three Renaissance Artists*
EDITH WHARTON · *Souls Belated*
WALT WHITMAN · *Song of Myself*
OSCAR WILDE · *The Portrait of Mr W. H.*

ANONYMOUS WORKS

Beowulf and Grendel   *Buddha's Teachings*
Gilgamesh and Enkidu   *Krishna's Dialogue on the Soul*
Tales of Cú Chulaind   *Two Viking Romances*